Owen AND Eleanor

Make Things Up

Book 2

Written by H.M. Bouwman • Illustrated by Charlie Alder

For Sierra. Welcome to the family!
—H.M.B.

Owen and Eleanor Make Things Up
Copyright © 2018 Sparkhouse Family. All rights reserved. No part of this
book may be reproduced without the written permission of the publisher.
Email copyright@1517.media.

First edition published 2018
Printed in the United States of America
25 24 23 22 21 20 19 18   1 2 3 4 5 6 7 8

Paperback ISBN: 9781506448459
Hardcover ISBN: 9781506449371
Ebook ISBN: 9781506448466

Illustrations by Charlie Alder
Cover design by Alisha Lofgren, 1517 Media
Interior design by Eileen Engebretsen, 1517 Media

Library of Congress Control Number: 2018949842

V63474; 9781506448459; OCT2018

Sparkhouse Family
510 Marquette Avenue
Minneapolis, MN 55402
beamingbooks.com

Chapter 1
Owen

Owen and Eleanor fought the evil space aliens, trying to keep them from attacking Earth and eating all their friends— and everyone else on the entire planet, including all the people they'd never even met. It was hard work saving the world. When Owen's light saber poofed into dust as he battled a tall alien with twenty arms, they decided to take a break.

"Freeze!" yelled Eleanor.

Owe picked up his sword. The stick had snapped right in half, but the pool noodle that went around its base was fine. "My laser still works," said Owen. "I just need a new sword part." He was panting. Fighting twenty-armed aliens was tiring.

"Anyway, I haven't read your true-life story yet," said Eleanor. "And you read mine as soon as I got home from school. So I think we should go upstairs and read yours. Also, maybe your place has some cookies? And some lemonade?"

It still felt like summer, hot and sticky, even though Eleanor had started second grade a whole week ago. Owen missed her when she was at school. He had lots of homeschool things to keep him busy, and he had his little brother Michael to do them with. But playing with Michael just wasn't the same as playing with Eleanor. Eleanor had been his friend ever since she moved into the bottom floor of his duplex, and he could lean out his window and yell down to her window and he could send her notes on the pulley system they'd built. She was the best friend he'd ever had.

But that didn't mean he wanted her to read—

"Your story?" said Eleanor. "Upstairs?"

He nodded gloomily. It was only fair, after all. He'd read her story. But hers was exciting, and his wasn't. Everyone in Eleanor's class had been told to write a true story about themselves, and to make it interesting. They had to keep a journal and write in it every day, and at the end of the week they were supposed to write a story about something real from their journal.

The true story was due in less than two weeks. And Eleanor's teacher told her class that they could enter their stories in a big contest at the library. The winner would get a coupon to the movie theater. Yesterday when Eleanor came home from school, she told Owen all about it, and Owen decided it would be fun to do the same homework and enter the library contest with her.

No, actually, *Eleanor* decided it would be fun if they both wrote true stories and both did the contest, but after she said it, Owen thought she was right. And Owen's dad, who was in charge of teaching him reading and writing, agreed. So Owen's homework was to write a true story now too. They had a week and a few extra days to write it and to make it really good.

Eleanor had already written two whole pages in her journal about how she ran away from home (which was actually true) and about how, when she ran away, she had also stopped a bank robbery and survived a flood and a hurricane, and met Wonder Woman and saved all the kids on a bus that was just about to plunge into a fiery canyon. Those parts were not actually one hundred percent true.

Their town did not even have a fiery canyon, Owen was pretty sure.

But Eleanor's story was interesting.

Owen said, "I especially like the bus full of children part. But . . . weren't you supposed to write something that really happened?"

"Sure," said Eleanor, twirling her light saber. "I just spiced it up a little." She stabbed the twenty-armed alien one last time, her curls bobbing as she leapt at the gingko tree.

"Well . . . ," said Owen. He wanted to say that Wonder Woman and hurricanes were maybe a little more than spice. He wanted to say that people would know she made those parts up. And he also wanted to say how exciting her story was, even if it wasn't real.

But Eleanor was already running up the back stairs to his second-floor apartment. To read his boring boring story.

Chapter 2
Eleanor

Eleanor sat in Owen's room, on the edge of Michael's bunk (the bottom one in the room he and Owen shared) with Owen's notebook in her hand. Owen had been sent to get the mail from downstairs, so she started to read without him. His story wasn't really a story. It was a list of all the things they'd done that summer—Eleanor moving in, the dead goldfish, the games they played, the books he'd read with his dad, the number of times he'd been to the ice cream store (four) and the flavors he'd eaten (chocolate, coconut, strawberry, and chocolate again). It needed a story. More like hers.

But Owen was right—her own story was too made up. She might have been able to convince people of either a hurricane or a flood or Wonder Woman, but *all* of them sounded—well, like she was exaggerating just a little. Maybe . . . maybe what they needed to do was come up with a story that was cool and interesting, but less fake-sounding? They needed something really good to write about.

Suddenly something under the bed bumped her foot, and she jumped. A snake? She scooted up the ladder to the top bunk.

Michael, who was five, stuck his head out from under the bed. "Is endless winter over? Is it Christmas yet? Where are Mr. and Mrs. Beaver?" He was playing Narnia again. He didn't even wait for an answer before crawling back under the bed.

Owen came into the room slowly. It had taken him a super-long time to get back. He carried a bright flier and was studying it as he walked, reading in little mutters. Then he stopped. "Hey, do you know this word?"

Eleanor slid down the ladder and scanned the paper. It was an ad. There was a photo of a bunch of kids wearing black uniforms and different colors of belts tied at their waists, kicking high in the air. They looked happy.

Some of the words said "One week free!" and "Kids' classes!" And there were some smaller words. And one big word that Eleanor couldn't read.

"This word," said Owen, pointing to the same word she didn't know.

She scrunched up her face and thought about it. "Maybe something that has to do with getting married?"

"With kicking? And kids our age?" said Owen.

"Maybe something that has to do with stores. You know: Mart."

"Mart can be a boy name too," said Owen.

"Oh!" said Eleanor suddenly. "Martians!"

Michael's voice rose from under the bed, muffled. "Dad knows all the words."

That was true. Owen and Michael's dad was a writer.

Eleanor looked closer at the ad. The free class started on Monday. And whatever this class was, it looked exciting. Like anything might happen here—something with marriage or stores or boy names or (best of all) Martians, and definitely something with kicking and cool costumes. This class might be exactly what they needed: something exciting to write about. Like a spy agency or an alien-fighting academy.

"We need to do this thing," she said.

"Let's ask my dad," said Owen.

As they left the room, Eleanor could hear Michael's voice rise from the floor again: "Ask the beavers. They'll know when Christmas is."

Chapter 3
Owen

Owen's mom and dad said yes, and so did Eleanor's. They could take the free class for one week. It turned out to be a martial arts class, which meant kicking and punching and things like that. It would start in just three days.

"Fighting!" whispered Eleanor in an awed voice. "Perfect." None of the parents heard her, which Owen thought was probably a good thing.

Owen and Eleanor were sitting in Eleanor's apartment with Goldfish, their silky orange kitten. Goldfish lived at Eleanor's, but she belonged to both of them.

Right now she was asleep on Owen's lap, and Owen was thinking about how wonderful a cat was and trying to think of the words for how its fur felt. Like . . . like . . . what did kitten fur feel like, exactly? Like brand new baby grass? No, it was softer than that. . . .

Eleanor said, "Will she ever be ready?"

"What?" said Owen. "She's sleeping."

"Not Goldfish. Alicia." Then Eleanor yelled, waking the kitten. "Da-ad! Can we walk to the library by ourselves? Please? We know the way completely by heart."

Eleanor's dad's voice drifted out of his bedroom (which was also his office). He was grading papers for the college class he taught. "You are not allowed to walk there by yourself. You know that."

They were still in a little bit of trouble because of running away in the summer. They weren't allowed to walk anywhere by themselves right now.

"Ugh!" said Eleanor. Goldfish stalked away to find somewhere quieter. "Alicia, hurry up!"

Alicia muttered something from her and Eleanor's bedroom. Owen was pretty sure it wasn't something completely polite.

But Eleanor didn't seem to notice. She had pulled out the flier from her dress pocket and was studying it. "Hey, did you see this part?" Slowly she read it out loud. "There will be a demon . . . a demonstration on the last day of class." She looked up at Owen. "That's a show. We're going to put on a show after we learn kung fu!"

"I'm not sure it's kung fu," said Owen. "It doesn't say kung fu anywhere."

"Whatever," said Eleanor. "We are going to have the best show in the class. Owen, we need to work on it starting now, so that we have something spectacular! This demo is something we can write about for our real-life stories—we'll win the demo and then win the writing contest too!"

"You know you can't both win," said Alicia, emerging from the bedroom.

"We'll tie," said Eleanor.

Owen nodded. A tie sounded good. But a show sounded kind of scary.

"Is Millie coming too?" asked Eleanor. Millie was Alicia's best friend, kind of like Owen and Eleanor, and she usually came to the library with them.

Alicia said, "No—I think she's busy." She didn't look at Eleanor when she answered. "Let's go, squirts."

"Don't call us squirts," said Eleanor. "We're karate champions. And right now I think we're too busy practicing our routine to go to the library—"

"Uh-uh," said Alicia. "No. It's my job to take you to the library, and I'm taking you now. Let's get it over with."

Owen said, "The class might not be karate. We can research martial arts at the library." He wanted to go to the library. It had Star Wars books that he'd never even read before. And once there was a dog that you could read to. And there was a librarian with short dreads and a pierced nose and a kind smile, and another librarian with the longest fingernails he'd ever seen, and when she typed she made comforting clicking noises on the keyboard. He always said hi to the librarians. And the dogs if there were any there.

Before leaving the duplex, they ran upstairs to get Michael, who was going with them. Really, Alicia was babysitting Michael, not Eleanor and Owen. At least that's what Eleanor said.

Michael held Alicia's hand to cross the streets, and as they walked, he told Alicia all about how beavers had giant flat tails and could slap the water. Eleanor and Owen walked behind, and Eleanor told Owen all about how they would win the demo.

When they got to the library, Alicia went with Michael to help him find books about beavers. Eleanor and Owen looked for books about martial arts.

They started by searching all the shelves. But pretty soon they got tired of that. There were way too many books, and the book covers didn't always say exactly what they were about. So they asked the librarian with the short dreads, and he helped them find the sports shelf. There was a whole sports shelf!

They found five martial arts books with lots of pictures. Eleanor said if they read them all, they would know all the martial arts by the end of the weekend. The nice librarian nodded and said, "Maybe you want a video too?"

He found them the Power Rangers. Owen hadn't ever watched the show before, and neither had Eleanor, but on the DVD cover the Power Rangers looked like really good martial artists. Eleanor's favorite was the Ranger in the pink costume, and Owen's favorite was the red.

That weekend they spent all their free time training (as Eleanor called it) for martial arts class. They read their five books to try to learn all the kicking and punching. Mostly they looked at the pictures and tried to do what the pictures showed. They watched three episodes of *Power Rangers*, which was the most their parents would let them watch. They practiced their kicks and punches in the backyard—and their jumping twirls like in *Power Rangers*.

And they each came up with a pose, which they noticed was very important for the Power

Rangers. Eleanor's pose was one fist over her head and one fist straight out in front of her, and one foot on its tiptoes ready to kick. Owen's pose was crouching like a tiger, with his hands in claws in front of him. Before they started their practices, they did their poses.

The only time they were not training was when they were eating or sleeping or going to church. It was a busy weekend.

By Monday they were ready to fight. And, as Eleanor said, they were ready to win the demo, make up a true story that would be worthy of fame, and win the writing contest.

We went to the library. The worker with the twisty dreads in his hair is named Shayne. He is six feet tall! (I asked him.) We asked him to help us find videos and he helped us. He's a grown-up. He has braces like Eleanor's brother Aaron but Shayne's are almost invisible. He's nice.

I wonder why Alicia's best friend Millie didn't come to the library with us.

Owen

27

The amazing Kung
fu fighters steal the
magical training book
from the ancient library!
They learn all the deep
secrets of the magic book!!

They win the demo with super-flying
kicks!!! The pink fighter is amazing and
the red fighter is really almost as good!
WHO ARE THESE HEROES? THEY
DEFEAT ALL THE BAD GUYS AND SAVE
THE DAY!

Eleanor

Chapter 4
Eleanor

On Monday Alicia walked them to the martial arts school— the dojo, Eleanor explained to her. It was a word they had learned from their library books.

When they walked in the front door of the dojo, they saw Alicia's friend Millie wearing a black uniform with a blue belt. "Millie!" Eleanor shouted. "Hi! I forgot you do karate!"

"It's not karate," said Millie, but she said it nicely. "And you have to talk in a quiet voice here. Like in school." She paused. "Hi, Alicia."

Alicia muttered, "Hi," and went to sit down on a bench right next to the door.

Millie shrugged, but she didn't look super-happy. "Okay. First, take your shoes and socks off. Everyone trains barefoot here."

"We know," said Eleanor. "We read some books this weekend. We also know all the kicks and punches—"

"Wow," said Owen. "Your hair is really cool."

Eleanor stared. Millie had a blue stripe in her dark hair. You could see it perfectly whenever she turned her head. Eleanor had never seen the blue stripe before, and it kind of made her wonder if maybe she hadn't seen Millie in a while.

"Thanks," said Millie. "I got it last week." She glanced at Alicia, but Alicia was pretending to read her book. Eleanor knew Alicia was only pretending because she was frowning like she was really smart and studying hard, and she never made that frown when she was really reading. Besides, she was reading a story about twins who babysat a lot, and Eleanor was pretty sure you didn't need to frown to understand that book.

Eleanor and Owen took off their shoes and socks and put them near Alicia's bench where other shoes and socks were lined up. The room they were in was big with almost nothing in it, just some giant bags at the end of the room that looked like you might kick them, and some folded-up mats that looked like you might do rolls and cartwheels on them. On the side of the room there was a door marked "Restrooms" and a door marked "Office." That was all. It didn't look the way Eleanor thought it should look. Where were the obstacles to leap over as they fought? The weapons? The uniforms? Did they get to pick a color like the Power Rangers?

There were six kids there besides Eleanor and Owen and Millie, all sitting on the floor with bare feet. Eleanor wanted to show off her pose and kicks and twirls, but the other kids were all bigger, and two of them even had black uniforms with yellow belts. She recognized the two kids from school: they were in third grade, a whole year older than her. Kimi and Derrick. Somehow it was harder to do poses and kicks and twirls in front of big kids in uniforms.

She asked Millie, "Will we get our uniforms today?"

Millie shook her head. "You'll borrow uniforms for the demo. You only get uniforms for keeps if you sign up for the class after the free week." She talked like she knew all kinds of things. Eleanor wasn't used to that. Usually Millie didn't know everything. Usually she was just a friend of Alicia's.

"Can I have a uniform with a blue belt?" It looked better than yellow, she thought. Older.

Millie grinned. "No, you have to earn that, after lots of practice. You'll have a white belt when you start. That means you're a beginner."

"What about yellow?" asked Eleanor, hoping that yellow was even more beginner than white.

"Yellow is the belt after white."

"Then blue?" asked Owen. When Millie nodded, Owen said, "You must have worked really hard."

"How quick can I get blue?" asked Eleanor. "Can I do it by the end of the week?"

Alicia, sitting in the chairs, snorted. They all turned to look at her, but she wasn't looking at them. She flipped a page in her book and kept frowning in a very smart way.

Kimi answered Eleanor's question. "It takes a really long time just to get a yellow belt. Months and months."

This class did not seem like a way to make Eleanor's and Owen's lives into an exciting story by the end of the week. You had to work super-hard just to get a yellow belt like Kimi and Derrick. And as far as Eleanor could tell, Kimi and Derrick were just normal third graders. She'd never seen them do anything remotely death-defying on the playground or in the lunchroom, except the day that Derrick put a whole sandwich in his mouth at one time. Eleanor wanted more than a sandwich.

To start class, the teacher came into the room and lined them up—with the yellow belts and Millie on one end because they knew more than everyone else. Eleanor leapt into her Power Ranger pose. She looked at Owen next to her, and slowly he got into his pose too. The teacher tipped his head at them and said, "Stand up straight, please. Hands at sides." Kimi made a little giggle.

The teacher had a black uniform with a black belt, which was probably the best color of all. He told them this school was called a dojo. But he said it wrong. He said it like this: "doh-jAHng."

Eleanor raised her hand. "Don't you mean a dojo?"

The teacher stared at her for a minute. So did the yellow belts and Millie. Then the teacher said, "No, that's the Japanese term. This is a Korean martial arts school, and we say dojang."

Eleanor decided just to listen for a little while.

The teacher taught them how to show respect by bowing and showed them how to stretch and told them to call him sir or Master Green and to call each other sir or ma'am.

Ugh. When would they start fighting?

Then Master Green said, "This is not a fighting class. That is the most important thing I can teach you today. This is a class about respect."

Ugggh. Eleanor was already learning respect and how to be a good person at home and at school and at church. Did she really need more goodness? She sat down on the mat.

"Stand up, please. Let's start with some kicking."

They kicked, and they punched, and they talked about respect and not fighting. Eleanor liked it all except the talking part. Then at the end of class, Master Green told them they needed to clean their rooms before the next day's class.

Ugggggggh.

Eleanor hoped Alicia hadn't heard anything, but on the way home, Alicia said, "Now you have to keep your side of the room clean."

Eleanor scowled, but Owen shrugged. His room was always pretty clean because their dad had a pick-up time every morning. Sometimes Owen and Michael picked up their toys more than once in a day. That was the main part of homeschooling that did not sound good to Eleanor. She only had to clean her room on Saturdays. She was glad her parents didn't know about Master Green.

"I'm going to tell Mom and Dad," said Alicia.

Uggggggggh.

They walked into Eleanor's apartment, and her dad gave them each an apple. Eleanor and Owen took their apples to the living room while Alicia stood in the kitchen talking to their dad. Eleanor heard Alicia say ". . . clean their rooms . . ." and sighed.

Owen said, "I can help you right now."

They picked up everything on Eleanor's side of the room. Alicia's side was already clean except for a small pile of books on her desk. Eleanor didn't have a desk on her side, but she did have a closet with shelves for toys and books, so she and Owen shoved everything in the closet and squeezed the door shut. Goldfish the orange cat swatted at the toys as they tossed them in the closet.

"Well," said Eleanor, "the class was fun"—she front-kicked and fell over—"but cleaning my room is less fun, and not learning fighting is no fun at all."

"I think pretend fighting is okay," said Owen. "Like in the backyard. I think we're just not supposed to beat people up."

"Huh," said Eleanor. "Huh huh huh." She was thinking. "We're going to need a super-great demo with fighting that is almost real, so that we can write about it for our essays and still win the demo and win the writing contest."

"Almost real fighting?" said Owen.

"So that everyone thinks it's real. We need it to be exciting." She kicked again and fell over again. This time she yelled to make the fall look like it was on purpose. "Boom! Like that, see?"

"That . . . makes sense," said Owen.

"When we win the demo, then we can win the writing contest too."

At martial arts class we learned to speak Korean. Dojang! And we learned front kick. Pow! We are going to win the demo!

Our uniforms will be black. Really, a pink belt would be better than white. Maybe I'll tell Master Green. He's the teacher. It takes more than a year to become a martial arts master but I think maybe it can go faster if you're a kid and have library books too. Grown-ups are slower learners.

Eleanor

Millie is in our martial arts class. She is the best jumper and kicker in the whole class—except for the teacher. And she has a blue stripe in her hair that she just got last week. She looked kind of sad when Alicia didn't talk to her or say anything nice about her hair. Millie and Alicia are best friends but Alicia is acting like they are not.

Owen

Chapter 5
Owen

On Tuesday afternoon, Alicia brought them to class again. This time she brought her purse, with her book and also her phone. It wasn't a real phone. It was an old one that used to belong to Eleanor's parents, and it couldn't make phone calls. It could only do text messages and internet, and only if there was Wi-Fi. Still, it looked like a real phone.

Alicia didn't even say hi to Millie. She just kind of waved halfway and then dropped her hand and sat down on the bench and got her phone out and started messing with it. She looked important and busy.

Millie waved back at Alicia, but Alicia didn't see her. Millie's shoulders dropped down a little, and she looked sad. Then she smiled at Owen and Eleanor and reminded them to take off their shoes and asked them how their day had gone at school.

Eleanor said, "We had dodgeball in gym today and Stella got hit in the face really hard. And it was pizza day and two kids bumped into each other with their trays and their pizza flew onto the floor."

"Cool," said Millie. "How was school for you, Owen?"

"Owen doesn't go to school," Eleanor reminded Millie. "He just does homework at home."

The way Eleanor said it, his life sounded boring. "I do too go to school," said Owen. "Homeschool. Today Michael and I made a volcano out of paper mache with our dad. We're going to finish it tomorrow." That wasn't actually completely true. They'd planned to make a volcano, but they went to the park first to meet some friends and then they ate lunch and cleaned up and did math and read a book and watched a Spanish video, and then the day was over and Owen's dad said they'd make the volcano tomorrow.

Unlike Owen, Eleanor was so *interesting.*

Dodgeball and people got hit in the face! Pizza and it fell on the floor! She probably wouldn't want to be Owen's friend if she knew he just played in the park and read books and stuff.

Eleanor's eyes got big. "A volcano? I have to see it tonight! Can it blow things up?"

"It's . . . not done yet. I'll show you when it's done tomorrow. Then we can blow things up together."

Suddenly Millie said something that was maybe in Korean, and everyone stood with their hands on their belts as the teacher walked into the room, and then everyone bowed. Owen and Eleanor bowed too, and Millie grinned at them to show they had done a good job figuring out what to do.

In class, Owen and Eleanor learned more kicking and punching. Eleanor, it turned out, was really good at ki-yapping, which is like yelling, but it is something you are *supposed* to do. Every time they kicked and punched, Eleanor yelled the loudest. Owen was less good at ki-yapping but he was good at kicking without falling over. Eleanor punched the bag really hard, and Owen jumped really high. They made a good team because they were each good at different things.

They also learned how to say thank you in Korean, and Master Green told them to pick up their rooms and be polite and not fight. That was a lot to remember.

Then Master Green said, "As you know,

there will be a demo at the end of the week. Tell your family to come and watch. It will be at the end of class on Friday."

Eleanor bounced up and down on her toes. She was so excited she looked like a volcano about to explode.

Owen felt more like a person who sees lava coming and needs to run away from it.

Eleanor said, "What's the prize if you win the demo? Is it a black belt?"

Master Green stared at Eleanor a long time, like he was thinking about a bunch of different things. Owen heard Kimi giggle and Millie say shhh to her quietly, but he didn't turn and look at them. He watched Master Green. How *did* you win the demo? What would he have to do in front of everyone to help Eleanor win?

"It's not a contest," said Master Green finally. "There isn't any winning, except that you try hard to put on a great show. That's what a demo is. We're going to put on a great performance. As a class we can show our kicks and punches, and the yellow belts can show some of their forms and techniques. And Millie can do a board break. How does that sound?" He smiled over at Kimi and Derrick and Millie.

Millie can do a board break? Owen had no idea she was so amazing.

"Owen and I can do something special too," said Eleanor. "We can break boards too."

"No, you can't," said Master Green. "Not until you're a blue belt. But if you two want to do something together, I bet we can figure out a routine for you tomorrow."

After everyone bowed and Owen and Eleanor got their shoes on, Alicia stood up and tucked her phone in her back pocket. "Let's go, munchkins."

Eleanor gritted her teeth. "I'm . . . not . . . a . . . munchkin."

Alicia's phone buzzed, and she pulled it out and looked at it.

"A text?" said Owen.

"From my friends." Alicia smirked at the text like it was something funny and then put the phone back in her pocket.

"You mean from Millie?" said Owen as they headed out the door.

Alicia looked surprised. "No, my *friends*. Who have phones and can text me."

"Did you hear that part in class about how Millie can break boards?" Owen said. He was asking Eleanor, but he also wanted to know what Alicia thought.

Eleanor said, "We need to get her to teach us. I wonder if she blasts through them with her fists or if she kicks them to smithereens with her bare feet."

"I bet she yells really loud. I mean, ki-yaps. I bet it looks really awesome."

"Could you guys hurry up?" said Alicia. "I need to get home so I can return this text."

"Do your other friends know Millie?" said Owen. Eleanor looked interested in the question too.

"Of course. She goes to our school." She paused like she was thinking about what to say. "They think her hair looks weird."

"It looks super cool," said Eleanor. "But even if it did look weird, who cares?"

Alicia said, "That shows what you know. There's a whole text thread about Millie's hair."

"Did you tell them they're all stupid?" said Eleanor.

Alicia rolled her eyes. "You don't know anything about how sixth grade works."

That was true, thought Owen, for both him and Eleanor. Then he thought about how second grade worked. He thought about their writing project. How was he going to write an exciting story that Eleanor would like? How would he keep her as a friend if he couldn't be more interesting—even more interesting than blue hair and breaking boards?

Maybe someday Eleanor would sit on a bench across the room from him and text her other friends—her *real* friends—and he would be all by himself.

I wish I didn't have to win a demo. It's a performance and I don't like performing very much. Anyway, we can't win the demo because it's not a contest. I need to find something I can do that's not in front of everyone but still interesting. So that Eleanor will stay my friend.

It seems like Alicia doesn't really like Millie anymore. I don't know why, because Millie is nice

and I know she still wants to be friends with Alicia. I can tell from the way she looks across the room at her when we are in martial arts class. But Alicia doesn't look back.

Owen

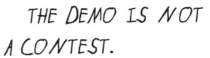

THE DEMO IS NOT A CONTEST.

What are we going to do???????????????????

We need a new plan. We can still win the writing contest. That is something real that you can win. There are movie tickets and everything. And THE FAME OF WINNING!!!

New plan: We don't have to win the demo. We just need to use our martial arts powers to defeat a bad guy. That will make a winning story!

New mission: find a bad guy to defeat.

Eleanor

Chapter 6
Eleanor

Eleanor thought about praying to God for a bad guy so that she and Owen could defeat him. But she didn't want a *super*-bad guy. Just *kind*-of-bad: bad enough to look scary but not so bad that she and Owen couldn't win in a fight against him. Maybe they needed a villain who was not very strong. Eleanor and Owen weren't quite completely experts at martial arts yet. She still fell over on a lot of her kicks.

But if the bad guy didn't know about the falling over, and if he wasn't completely a martial artist himself, he'd be terrified by her Power Rangers pose. She had a great pose. And so did Owen when he got into it.

This could work.

She was thinking so hard that when it was time to pray at supper, she didn't even think about adding the bad guy into the prayer until after praying was all over. So she closed her eyes again and said it in her head: *Dear God, please send me a bad guy who is scared of my Power Ranger pose.*

"What are you doing?" said Alicia. "Time to eat, weirdo."

"Absolutely no calling names," said Mom.

"I was saying an extra prayer," said Eleanor. "If you must know." It made Eleanor feel like a holy person, like she was more religious than Alicia. She sat up straight and tried to look extra-good. Like someone who said extra prayers.

Alicia's phone buzzed from her pocket.

Mom held out her hand, palm up, and Alicia turned the phone off and gave it to her. They weren't supposed to have electronics at the table. It didn't matter to Eleanor since she didn't have any electronics, but Alicia and Aaron sometimes forgot.

"She had her phone at the dojang too," said Eleanor. Alicia wasn't supposed to carry it around with her. She was only supposed to use it for one hour or less per day, and only after homework.

Alicia glared at Eleanor.

"You can have it back tomorrow," said Mom.

"What?!"

"You heard your mom," said Dad. "It doesn't seem like you're obeying the phone rules."

"Because the rules are dumb," said Alicia.

Eleanor could not believe she said that.

"All my other friends get to use their phones whenever they want. And they have *real* phones," said Alicia.

"Millie doesn't have a phone," said Eleanor. "And she has cool blue hair," she added. Mom would be interested.

"Be quiet!" said Alicia.

Aaron said, "We have a big math test tomorrow. On vectors. Want to know what those are?"

"Yes," said Mom. "What are vectors?"

"And please pass the rolls." Dad winked across the table at Mom.

The rest of the meal was all about vectors, which, as far as Eleanor could see, were kind of like arrows moving quickly up a hill. Or moving down a hill, but either way, always moving, running forward and headed somewhere.

That didn't seem like math exactly. It seemed more like a good explanation for how Eleanor was always charging forward. She was a vector. And Owen . . .

Suddenly she had a thought: Owen wasn't like a vector, and that was a nice thing about him. He was good at sitting still and thinking. But for defeating a bad guy, she needed him to charge forward. So she'd have to drag him along. She would be the vector.

In martial arts class on Wednesday they learned cartwheels! And weird rolls—not like in gymnastics class at all. And how to fall. How to fall! Eleanor loved that best of all.

First of all, you could pretend you were slipping on ice, or thrown from a truck, or dropped into a fiery canyon, and second of all, you were supposed to yell—ki-yap, that is—on the way down. What could be more fun?

Near the end of class, Master Green called them all over. "What are some things you would like to do for the demo?"

"Owen and I," said Eleanor, "are going to show how to defeat a bad guy. How to fight him off."

Master Green looked at Eleanor a long time, like he was thinking lots of big thoughts. Maybe he was thinking about how amazing she'd be in a fight.

Then he nodded. "Okay. Eleanor and Owen can do a short sparring demo. That's pretend fighting. You will not actually be kicking and punching each other. You're not advanced enough to do that. One person will hold a focus pad and the other person will kick it." He gestured to Millie, who brought him a kicking pad that you could hold in your hand. Then he and Millie showed Eleanor and Owen how to hold it so the other person could kick it. "This pad is your target," he said. "You two should come up with a routine of kicks and punches—maybe three or four kicks and punches each. Next class, we'll work on it."

"We just kick and punch the pad?" said Eleanor.

"That's right."

Well. This sparring demo was not going to be the amazing fight Eleanor had been imagining. She would have to come up with something more.

Chapter 7
Owen

 After class, Alicia was not sitting on the bench. She wasn't anywhere. They stood outside the dojang, not sure what to do. "We should wait," said Owen. They weren't supposed to walk home alone, not after the running-away incident that summer.

Eleanor frowned. "Our parents need to know that we're big kids and can obey rules. We should walk home and prove it to them."

"Uh . . . the rule right now is to *not* walk home alone."

But Eleanor didn't seem to be listening anymore. She was staring at a car across the street, parked in front of the bank in a no-parking spot. There was a man sitting in the car, talking on his phone. The car was running.

"Is that someone you know?" said Owen.

Eleanor shook her head. "That," she said, "could be a getaway car."

"What?"

"Wouldn't it be the perfect place to park if you were a bank robber? The other robber goes inside while you wait in the car."

"The other robber?"

"Your partner in crime. Your accomplice."

Owen knew that word. His dad used it sometimes when he talked about Owen and Eleanor getting into trouble together.

Then an old, old man walked slowly out of the bank. He used two canes to walk. The man in the car put down his phone, got out, and helped the old, old man into the car. Then they drove off.

"Well, it *could* have been a bank robber," said Eleanor.

"Let's go," said Alicia. She had been in the bathroom. They started walking home.

"I bet," muttered Eleanor, so that Alicia couldn't hear, "that tomorrow there will be a bank robber parked out there. And we'll stop him. With our martial arts skills and our giant brains. *That* will be something to write a winning story about."

Owen was pretty sure Eleanor couldn't predict a robbery tomorrow. But he decided to wait until tomorrow and see. With Eleanor, you never knew.

On Wednesdays, Owen and Michael usually did Activities Night at Eleanor's church. It wasn't a church service. It was supper and classes. Owen's family didn't go to Eleanor's church normally, but Owen and Michael went there on Activities Night so their dad could write his next book.

First, they had spaghetti supper in the church basement for three dollars per kid. After eating, they went to classes. Eleanor's dad, who knew Spanish because he grew up in Costa Rica, went to teach a Spanish class for grown-ups. Eleanor's mom went to another grown-up class, and Alicia went upstairs for choir. Michael went to make crafts with the little kids. Owen and Eleanor went to a cooking class with the medium-sized kids.

Owen liked cooking class. Today they learned to make big pretzels, and they had a lesson about how the arms of the pretzels are folded, which can remind you how to pray. Owen asked where the pretzels were in the Bible, but the cooking teacher said they didn't have pretzels in Bible times. Owen thought about how Bible-times people had to pray without their hands folded. He guessed that wasn't too bad, as long as they could still pray.

"They could still pray, though, right?" he said.

The teacher said yes. Anyone could pray, whenever they wanted to talk to God.

Owen wondered if he should pray that there would be no bank robbers tomorrow. Or maybe he should pray that he would be interesting enough for Eleanor to keep liking him but without having to fight criminals who wanted to rob banks.

When the pretzels were in the oven, he asked to go to the bathroom. Eleanor and the other kids were playing a guessing game. It was a little too loud for Owen. He took a long time walking to the bathroom, and on the way back he snuck upstairs to the big room with all the benches where everyone sat on Sunday. The choir was in the front of the big room, and they didn't see Owen in the back, in the dark. The choir director was talking quietly—Owen couldn't hear his words—and the choir people were all listening. Some of them were grown-ups, and a few were older kids like Alicia. She was in the second row, and she looked serious and nice and not like someone who made fun of people with blue hair.

Owen stared up at the big organ pipes in the front of the church, on the wall behind the choir. He loved the pipes. Some of them were so big he could have crawled through them— except they went straight up. Others were small, like straws—and there were all sizes in between. The organ itself sat off to the side of the stage and reminded Owen of a spaceship, with a lot of controls and things to push in and pull out. He wasn't supposed to touch it.

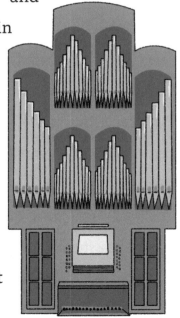

Owen's church didn't have an organ. It didn't have a big room like this, and it didn't have benches—just folding chairs. It was in a house, and there were donuts and juice before church but nothing after. And there was silent time, and listening to people's concerns, and singing with a guitar and a piano, but no organ. Owen always liked to sneak upstairs in Eleanor's church to look at the organ pipes. How do you play an organ, anyway? Would it feel like crossing hands and praying? Somehow he thought it might.

Sometimes the organist would be there practicing, and that was the best. Sometimes the organ sounded soft and gentle, and other times it sounded like yelling because you were happy, and other times it sounded like angry yelling. But it always sounded like something. Like it was talking somehow, to someone much bigger than Owen.

Maybe an organ would be something interesting to write about.

No, an organ was only interesting to Owen. He was pretty sure of that. He turned to go back to the loud kitchen.

And suddenly the choir started singing. First they were just humming, and then one voice rose up out of the humming, high and perfect, like an organ might sound if an organ was an angel. Owen's mind and heart felt all mixed up. The sound was so beautiful. There weren't any words he could understand—it was a different language. But he could tell what it was: a prayer.

He turned back to look.

The singer was Alicia. Singing like she loved everyone in the world.

Owen almost didn't remember going down the stairs after the song ended. His class was eating the folded-hands pretzels. Eleanor had saved him one. Then it was time to go, so they met Eleanor's family and walked home.

On the walk home, Eleanor told her mom and dad every detail of cooking class, even that Owen had asked a question out loud. She told them everything except about Owen's trip up to the choir and his thoughts, which were secret because no one knew about them except him. And God.

Then Eleanor's mom said, "It sounds like you two had a great time. Michael, what about you? What did you do?"

They were almost home. Michael said, "I did nothing." He didn't sound mad or sad.

"Oh? Why not?"

"The teacher told us to do acting. I don't do acting."

Eleanor said, "Acting is great!" She twirled.

And Eleanor's dad said, "But you're so good at pretend, Michael. I thought you would like acting."

Michael stood still and put his hands on his hips. Everyone stopped to look at him. He said, "Acting and pretending are not the same thing. Pretend is by yourself. Acting is in front of people. I don't like in front of people." Then he kept walking.

"Well," said Eleanor's mom. She had a little bit of laughter in her voice. "That makes sense."

Owen thought so too. All of a sudden, he saw that there were some ways that he and Michael were more the same than he and Eleanor. Eleanor was wonderful, but maybe Michael was wonderful sometimes too. Maybe Michael could be a friend too.

Especially if Eleanor didn't want to play with Owen anymore because he was too boring.

When they got home, Eleanor pulled Owen aside before he went up the stairs. She whispered, "Remember, tomorrow we stop the bank robbery. Be prepared."

Alicia seems like a nice person. She takes us to the library. She helps Michael find books on beavers. She listens when I talk to her. And when she sings, she sounds like she is singing right to God. I do not know why she is being mean to Millie. Because I really think she is.

And I'm worried that she's mean to Millie because Millie isn't interesting to her anymore.

And maybe Eleanor will feel like that about me someday too. I don't want to stop a bank robber, but maybe I need to so that Eleanor will stay my friend.

Owen

WHAT IS GOING WRONG WITH MY LIFE? If I can't make something really interesting happen, how will we win the writing contest? In order to win, your story needs to be the MOST EXCITING. Doesn't it??

I have to have to HAVE TO stop a bank robber tomorrow. But first there has to BE a bank robber. Doesn't there?

Eleanor

Chapter 8
Eleanor

On Thursday, Eleanor raced home from school. Owen was already in her apartment playing with the kitten. He had his journal with him. Eleanor got hers, too, so that they could write some notes after the bank robbery. The essay needed to be written soon: Eleanor's homework was due Monday. And for the contest, they had to bring their essays to the library before it closed on Monday night. That was only five days away if you counted today as a day. Eleanor tucked her journal into the pocket of her bright pink dress, and Owen carried his, because it was too big to fit in his pocket.

Eleanor's dad gave them each one chocolate chip cookie and one apple, and then he walked them to martial arts. Alicia would come to pick them up before the end of class.

"It's okay if she's late," said Eleanor. "We'll wait for her, just like we're supposed to." She tried to wink at Owen, but she wasn't very good at winking yet, so she just blinked a few times. Owen blinked back. With his glasses, he looked a little bit like an owl.

In class they practiced their kicks and punches so they would be ready for the demo. Then Master Green told them to break into groups to practice their special parts for the demo. Eleanor and Owen worked on their sparring routine.

First, Owen held the focus pad and Eleanor kicked. She did the flashiest front kick she could do, and then some punches with loud ki-yaps. Then Eleanor held the pad for Owen, and he did some kicks and punches.

But their routine wasn't exciting enough. Eleanor could see the two yellow belts practicing. Kimi twisted Derrick over her hip and threw him to the ground. He fell just like they had been taught to fall in class, slapping his arm on the mat—but it was *real* falling, with actually being thrown. Millie was in a corner, twirling a long stick like a giant baton. Even the other white belts looked cool, blocking the pool noodle that Master Green swung at them. Unless Owen and Eleanor did something better than they were doing now, they were not going to have the best demo.

"Stop," she said, just as Owen was about to practice his combination again. "This is no good."

"What do you mean?" said Owen.

"We need to make it more real, like we're

actually kicking and punching each other."

"But Master Green said—"

"We won't *really* kick and punch. We'll act."

"I don't like acting . . ."

"Then pretend, okay? When I kick, you jump back like I really kicked you. And we need better kicks." She thought for a minute. "I can do a cartwheel kick and then a flying kick. That will look awesome."

"A . . . *what* kind of kick? I don't think we learned those yet."

"I'm sure I can figure them out," said Eleanor. She'd practice in the backyard tonight. Or in her room after bedtime.

Just then, Master Green called for class to

finish, so they lined up with the other students to bow.

A few minutes later, when they got outside, Alicia wasn't there. Again.

Perfect!

Eleanor looked across the street. There was another car parked in the no-parking zone next to the bank. This one was black, exactly like a getaway car should be.

Owen nudged her. "Alicia's down the street."

Eleanor glanced over. Sure enough, there was Alicia, about a block away, walking quickly. She waved like she was telling them to wait for her.

Eleanor looked back at the car. Its engine

wasn't running but the flashers were on.

What are you thinking?" asked Owen. He sounded like he didn't exactly want to know.

Eleanor pointed. The woman in the driver's seat was leaning back against the headrest with her eyes closed.

"I don't think she's a robber," Owen said. "I think she's sleeping."

"That's to fool us," said Eleanor. Only the best bank robbers would park and then pretend to sleep. "She even turned the car off so it looks like she's not going anywhere in a hurry." She glanced back at Alicia, but Alicia was still more than half a block away, now looking down at her phone and walking slowly. "Come on!"

"What?" said Owen.

Eleanor was already rushing across the street. There weren't any cars coming—she checked first. "Hurry up." She turned from the middle of the street and waved Owen to follow. "We need to stop this tragedy from taking place."

When they got to the car, the woman didn't even look up. She had a tiny bit of drool on the side of her mouth.

"We're pretending, right?" said Owen. They both stood on the sidewalk right next to the car.

"We're not pretending. We're making something happen," said Eleanor. "This is how you get an exciting life that makes a good story. Owen, stay here on the sidewalk to stop the criminal from escaping the car before the police arrive."

"How do I stop her?"

"When she comes to the sidewalk, you can block her with your martial arts! I'll keep her from driving away with the loot."

At that moment, a man with a briefcase jogged past them and got in the passenger side. He said something to the woman and she woke up. He seemed to be telling her to hurry, but he was also laughing. She wiped the little drool mark off her face.

"The briefcase full of loot!" said Eleanor. "And he was running. This proves he's a robber!"

She leapt in front of the parked car. Owen stayed where he was to stop the woman from escaping. He put his arms out like a starfish. His journal lay on the ground next to his feet.

Eleanor starfished her arms too. "Halt, thieves!" she yelled in her loudest voice.

The woman started the car's engine.

Eleanor ki-yapped. Really really loud.

The woman looked at her, startled.

The man was still smiling but he looked confused. "Little girl," he called out the window, "you need to get out of the road."

Eleanor ki-yapped again. Even louder. Loud enough to bring the cops running. Owen stood with his arms out, and he did a much quieter ki-yap. It sounded almost like a yelp.

Suddenly there was a hand on Eleanor's shoulder and someone was pushing her off the road and onto the sidewalk.

It was Alicia.

Alicia looked angry. "What in the world are you doing?" She kept pushing Eleanor forward, even when Eleanor was clearly on the sidewalk, and she grabbed Owen's shirt collar as they walked past him. And now she was propelling them both down the sidewalk.

The car drove off. Eleanor said, "They were bank robbers!"

"I promise you they were not," said Alicia. "And I'm telling Mom and Dad." She stomped back to where Owen had dropped his journal on the ground and picked it up, stuffing it in her pocket so she could grab both their hands and drag them toward home.

"Fine," said Eleanor. "Then they'll know you were late to pick us up, and when they ask where you were, I'll tell them you were walking super-slow and staring at your phone." She could feel her eyes getting watery. This was their last chance to make something exciting happen, she just knew it. The demo

wasn't going to be awesome enough. The bank robbery was their last chance. Now Eleanor and Owen would end up writing terrible stories, and they wouldn't win the contest, and they would both fail second grade, and they would never do anything amazing in their lives ever.

Alicia glared and let go of them. "I guess I won't tell on you this time," she said. "But you better *never* stand in the road again." She stalked toward home, and they trailed behind her.

Owen said quietly, "I'm sorry about the bank robbery not going right."

"We're sunk," said Eleanor. "I'm out of ideas. Even a flying kick isn't going to be enough." She didn't know what to do. She was lost.

Owen was quiet for a long time. Then he said, in a low voice, like he was making a big decision, "I'll think of something. For the demo tomorrow. I'll think of something exciting. I promise."

Chapter 9
Owen

Eleanor came over later that afternoon to see Owen and Michael's volcano and to run lava over lots of Lego people. Mom, who was a paramedic, was working that whole day and night, so after Eleanor left at suppertime, it was just Michael and Dad and Owen at home.

It was Owen's turn to pray out loud. It was supposed to be Michael's turn, but Michael said he had prayed out loud at Wednesday church. At the end of his class he had prayed really loud for no more acting. He said even the teacher heard him.

So it was Owen's turn today. They were having homemade pizza, which was already on the table smelling delicious. It was Michael's favorite supper and one of Owen's favorites too, so he made sure to say thank you for pizza. Then he said, "And please give us interesting lives that we can write good stories about. Amen."

"Huh," said Dad as they each took a slice. "You know, there's an old legend about how you can curse someone by saying 'May you live in interesting times.' Why do you think that is?" He passed the salad bowl.

Owen took a helping of salad and passed it to Michael, who carefully placed one lettuce leaf on his plate. "I don't know," said Owen. He thought about the bank robbery. What if it had been a real robbery? "Maybe because interesting is sometimes scary."

Michael took two slices of pizza and picked all the mushrooms off both pieces, piling them next to the lettuce leaf.

"Dad," said Owen, "you don't put magical stuff or dragons in the books you write, so how do you make them interesting? I mean, the people in your books are just doing normal boring stuff, right?"

"Well," said Dad, "I just wrote a chapter about a family having dinner."

"Pizza?" said Michael.

"Soup."

Michael said, "Yep, pretty boring," and pressed his two pizza slices together like a sandwich. Sauce slid down his hands and chin.

Dad said, "To answer your question, Owen: when I write, I try to write something that seems like it could really happen in our world. Those are the kinds of stories I like to write—real-world stories. But even if a story is set somewhere make-believe—in Narnia, for example—the things that happen there have to *feel* like they really could happen, or the reader won't believe the story. They have to seem real."

Owen nodded, chewing his pizza slowly. If they couldn't make their lives interesting, they could at least make up an interesting story. But not like what Eleanor did with Wonder Woman and fiery canyons. That kind of made-up story wasn't going to fool anyone.

He thought about it all evening. When they went to bed, Michael fell asleep right away, but Owen, on the top bunk, had trouble sleeping. What could he do tomorrow? How could he keep Eleanor as his friend?

The problem with the bank robbery was that

Eleanor couldn't make it actually happen, even though she wanted to. And if they made up a bank robbery story, no one would believe them, because two kids finding and stopping bank thieves just didn't seem real.

He turned his pillow over, looking for the cool side.

He didn't want to lie. The story needed to be something almost true. Almost true wasn't lying, was it? Not like Wonder Woman and kids on a crashing bus.

So . . . what could he come up with that would be amazing and believable—and almost true?

And just before he drifted off to sleep, an idea came into his head. It was a little scary. It meant he would have to do acting. But it would be exciting, and it would impress Eleanor, and she would stay friends with him. She might even win the writing contest.

The almost-last thought he had before sleep was that he should write his idea down in his journal when he woke up. As he drifted off to sleep, it seemed like there was some reason he couldn't write in his journal, but he couldn't remember what that reason was.

The bank robbery wasn't a bank robbery. We almost got in trouble again, maybe even as bad as running-away kind of trouble.

Nothing is working right!

Tomorrow, Owen will save us. HELP ME, OWEN-WAN-KENOBI! YOU'RE MY ONLY HOPE!

Eleanor

Chapter 10
Eleanor

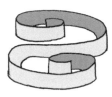Friday after school, Alicia walked Eleanor and Owen to martial arts class. At the end of class, they would do the demo. Eleanor didn't know what Owen had planned. They hadn't had a chance to be alone so that he could tell her. But Owen was smart. He'd come up with something amazing.

Alicia sat on the bench with her book. She didn't seem to have the phone with her today. When she saw Millie, she waved—not just one wave but two. Alicia looked like she wanted to say something important but she was too embarrassed to yell it across the room. Millie's eyebrows went way up, but then class started, so there wasn't time for any more surprise. There was just practicing for the demo and reviewing everything they'd learned that week.

Near the end of class, Eleanor and Owen went to work on their sparring routine, and Master Green came over to help them, which was great except it meant they didn't have time for Eleanor to hear Owen's amazing plan. What *was* it?

Master Green wanted them to do front kicks and straight punches and palm strikes on the pad. He said that would look good. It didn't look as good as flying kicks though—Eleanor was sure of it. But she also didn't know how to do a flying kick. She'd tried in the backyard last night—and she'd ripped a giant hole in her favorite pink leggings. Her flying kick was really not perfect.

Finally, Master Green turned away for just a minute to answer someone's question. Eleanor took the chance to whisper to Owen. "So—what's your plan? It's awesome, right?"

Owen nodded, but he looked serious and a little scared. "You just have to kick me in the stomach," he said. "A pretend kick, but make it look real."

Master Green was back. "Less chatting, kids. Let's run that drill again."

Near the end of class, Master Green loaned all the new kids black pants and a black t-shirt for the demo. They went in the bathrooms to change, and when they came out, there were people coming into the dojang, mostly parents but also some brothers and sisters and friends and even a few grandmas and grandpas. Eleanor's and Owen's parents were there, and also Michael and Aaron. And of course Alicia. There were so many people that they didn't have enough places to sit, even though Millie got some chairs out of a closet. Alicia gave her seat to a grandma-type of person, and she and Michael sat on the floor in front of the parents.

And then the demo started!

Chapter 11
Owen

First, the class all kicked and punched together. Then, the two yellow belts threw each other to the ground. Owen and Eleanor would be next.

Owen was nervous. He knew it was because he was about to do acting. In front of people. But even more, it was because he needed the plan to go well so that Eleanor would want to stay his friend.

He wasn't even paying attention to the yellow belt routine because he was so busy worrying. Suddenly Master Green said, "Now Eleanor and Owen will show some kicking and punching combinations."

Eleanor held the pad for Owen, who kicked and punched. He didn't do anything new or different, even though he could tell that Eleanor was expecting it. He really felt sick now. His stomach was all knotted up.

And then it was time for his plan.

As he took the focus pad from Eleanor, he whispered, "Do the cartwheel flying kick. I have a plan." He added, "Ma'am," because that's what they were supposed to call each other in class.

Her face lit up in a grin. "Yes, sir!" she whispered back.

And her kick was glorious. It was fantastic. It was truly sensational. She first did a Power Ranger pose—just a quick one, not showing off—and then she ran and cartwheeled and

did a jumping sidekick, and even though she fell at the end, it was amazing.

Part of the reason she fell, probably, was because Owen surprised her. This was his plan. Instead of backing away from the jumping sidekick so she could kick the pad, he moved forward, and she actually kicked *him*. Right in the stomach. He jumped right in her way. She didn't kick him hard—but she kicked him hard enough that Owen said, "Ooof."

Then Owen fell to the floor, too, holding his stomach and saying, "Oooooh." Groaning.

Eleanor jumped up and grabbed him. "Are you okay?"

Still groaning, he blink-blinked at her to show he was fine. He was pretending.

She blink-blinked back and made an "oh" with her mouth. Then she said, loudly and in a worried voice, "I think Owen broke his stomach! This is really serious."

Master Green came over and felt Owen's stomach and told him that he would be okay. Owen's mom—the paramedic—came and led him off the floor to sit by her. And the other students and parents looked worried.

Chapter 12
Eleanor

Millie did her twirling stick routine after that, and while people were watching Millie, Eleanor whispered to Owen, "This is all part of the plan, right?"

Owen nodded and clutched his stomach. Eleanor patted his shoulder like he was really injured.

At the end of the demo, Master Green asked everyone except Owen to bow, and he gave out fliers about classes to all the parents so they could sign their kids up for more than just the free week. But he looked a tiny bit sad, like everything hadn't gone exactly right. Eleanor wondered if maybe he wanted a demo with no broken stomachs.

Master Green came over as people were leaving and talked to Owen's parents. "Is Owen feeling better?"

Owen was still groaning a little and holding his stomach.

Owen's mom shook her head no. "I'm not sure what's going on. I think we might take him to the clinic. He doesn't usually overreact about getting hurt."

Master Green said, "That's a good idea. Please let me know what happens. Owen's been a great student. I'm sorry the week ended like this." He saw Eleanor and said, "Eleanor has been a wonderful student too."

"I didn't mean to kick him," said Eleanor. "I'm just stronger than I think." She felt a little guilty. She didn't know why—Owen wasn't really hurt, after all. He was just making the day more interesting. And they could both write a story about how she was so powerful that she sent someone to the hospital!

But . . . not Owen. You don't send your best friend to the hospital. No, they'd have to change that part so that Eleanor kicked a bad guy. Maybe a robber.

This story was getting really complicated.

Since Owen's mom knew lots of medical stuff, she drove him to the clinic. Eleanor went along to keep Owen company. In the waiting room, Owen's mom talked with the desk worker as they waited for a doctor, and Owen and Eleanor sat in some chairs near the coloring table.

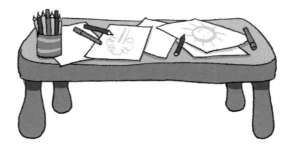

The coloring table was for kids Michael's age or even smaller. But even though it was for little kids, Eleanor studied it because some of the coloring papers looked kind of fun. And the crayons weren't all broken like at lots of places . . .

Wait. There were actually *markers* at the coloring table. What were the doctors thinking? Didn't they know little kids couldn't be trusted with markers?

Suddenly Eleanor had an idea. "Let me see your stomach."

Owen pulled up his shirt. "I'm actually fine," he whispered. "Remember my winking?" He looked a little worried.

"I know," said Eleanor. "But we need to make this story more real." She took a red marker and colored his stomach to make a bruise, then added a little bit of blue on the edges for when the bruise starts to turn colors. It was perfect. And nice and round, almost like a target.

"Mom's coming," whispered Owen.

Eleanor dropped the shirt and slid over to the coloring table to return the markers.

Owen's mom said, "There's a bit of a wait. Meanwhile, let me feel your stomach again." She pressed gently on it through Owen's shirt. "Does it hurt when I touch it?"

"OW," said Owen. "OW OW OW."

"Here?" said Owen's mom, moving her hand higher up on his stomach.

"OW," said Owen. "OWWWW." But to be honest, he did not sound that convincing. He wasn't the best actor.

Then Owen's mom pulled up his shirt and saw the giant round bruise.

She looked from Owen to Eleanor and back again.

"Well," she said. "What exactly are you two up to?"

Eleanor bobbed on her toes. "Owen's very very injured from my super-powerful sidekick," she said. "You can see the bruise."

"This is marker," said Owen's mom. She looked at the coloring table and sighed. "I'm going to take our name off the doctor list. And then we are leaving and you two can tell me what you think you're doing, making up a story like this."

Chapter 13
Owen and Eleanor

It turned out that going to the doctor was super-expensive, and if Owen's mom hadn't cancelled the appointment, it would have cost a lot more money than what they both had in their piggy banks. It also turned out that Owen saying he was injured when he wasn't was a lie. And Eleanor helping him do it was also a lie.

There were, it turned out, a lot of things that were lying. Telling stories for fun—if everyone knew they were made up—was okay. Like Owen's dad did for his writer job. But telling a story that was made up and pretending it was true was lying. Even if only *part* of it was made up. It was complicated.

They talked about everything at the ice cream shop near their duplex, where Owen's mom brought them on the way home. She liked to have serious talks whenever they did something wrong. But it was okay, because the talks usually also had ice cream or something nice.

"Why did you do it?" asked Owen's mom. "Why did you make up this story?"

"We needed something exciting to win the

story contest," said Eleanor. "At the library."

"The contest isn't for the most exciting things that happen," said Owen's mom. "It's for the most interesting story. And interesting comes from how it's written."

"What?" said Eleanor. "We haven't even started writing yet!"

"You have your journals," said Owen's mom. "You could write about stuff that's in your journal."

Eleanor nodded, thinking.

Owen's mom said, "You haven't said anything, Owen. Why did you tell the story about being injured?" She looked like she was waiting for more answer than what Eleanor gave.

And Owen decided to tell her the truth. "I was worried . . . ," he said. His mom and Eleanor both stared at him. Eleanor was listening so hard that her Superman ice cream was dripping down the cone and over her hand. "I was worried that Eleanor wouldn't be my friend. If I wasn't more interesting," he said quickly. "I don't care about winning the contest. I just want Eleanor to think I'm exciting and stay friends with me."

Now Eleanor's cone was dripping all over her dress and onto the floor. She stared at Owen. "I always think you're interesting!"

Owen's mom said, "You don't need to be extra-exciting to keep true friends. Just be yourself."

"Yourself is amazing," said Eleanor.

"But Millie . . ."

"You have volcanoes in your house! And we read Narnia books together and go in the closet and go to Narnia! And we get in trouble together!" (Owen's mom nodded.)

Eleanor looked like she was going to keep listing things, but suddenly the door to the ice cream shop opened and Alicia walked in—with Millie. They were talking and smiling.

Alicia stopped for a minute when she saw them. "Are you okay, Owen?"

"He's fine," said Owen's mom. "False alarm."

"That's good." Alicia reached into her purse. "Owen, I have your journal—I forgot to give it back to you yesterday." She held it out to him, and just before he took it, she said, "I . . . I read part of it. It was really good. It . . . helped me to see some things. Anyway, I'm sorry I read it without asking you."

Owen took the journal. "That's okay." He felt weird about her reading it, but he was glad it helped her. Maybe that's what true writing was really good for: helping people to see things that were important.

Alicia got in line with Millie for ice cream.

Owen's mom said, "There's still the demo to talk about."

Eleanor said, "We kind of ruined Master Green's demo." She licked her hand.

"Can we fix it?" said Owen.

Owen's mom handed Eleanor a napkin. "You can't change the demo anymore. But you can tell Master Green you're sorry."

"We could do a We're Sorry Demo," said Eleanor.

"I think you can *say* sorry to start with," said Owen's mom. "How's your ice cream?"

Owen took some quick licks to catch up on the drippiness of his. It was chocolate with marshmallow, which he'd never tried before. "It's good."

"Mine tastes just like Superman," said Eleanor. "But there really should be a Wonder Woman flavor too."

They wrote their true stories over the weekend. Eleanor wrote about moving into the duplex and meeting her best friend and having lots of imaginary battles with aliens. It was a mostly-happy story, with a dead goldfish and running away and coming home again. Owen wrote about taking martial arts class and making

up a fake story. It was a sad story in parts, and it didn't have an ending completely. He also wrote a story about seeing the organ at church and how organ music was like a folded-hands prayer. His dad said that one was not a story but a poem. So Owen wrote a poem without even realizing it. Eleanor said he was a genius.

On Monday Eleanor read her story to her class and everyone liked it. Monday after school, Eleanor's dad brought Owen and Eleanor to the library to turn in their stories for the contest. They gave the stories to the librarian with the dreads, and he read them (and Owen's poem) right then and said they were amazing and interesting. Owen grinned.

And Eleanor thought winning somehow didn't seem so important anymore.

Then Eleanor's dad took them to the dojang so they could say they were sorry for ruining the demo.

Master Green talked with them in his office. He had three chairs waiting for them to sit in, and he said he was glad for their apology because it meant they were being responsible. He also said they should clean their rooms. Eleanor's dad smiled.

Then Master Green handed Owen and Eleanor two packages and said, "Now you better put on your uniforms. Class starts in ten minutes."

Eleanor's dad said, "The parents talked

about it and we all decided we could afford two classes per week. You start today."

Ki-yap!

About the author:

In addition to the Owen and Eleanor stories, **H. M. Bouwman** writes historical fantasy for older kids, including *A Crack in the Sea* and *A Tear in the Ocean*. She is a Professor at the University of St. Thomas, a mom of two homeschooled kids, and a fifth-degree black belt in the traditional Korean martial art of Kuk Sool Won.

About the illustrator:

Charlie Alder has illustrated many books for children, including her first authored and illustrated picture book, *Daredevil Duck*. She describes herself as "a curly haired coffee drinker and crayon collector." She lives in Devon, England, with her husband and son.

Coming May 2019

A new kid moves into Owen and Eleanor's neighborhood, and she looks about the same age as Owen and Eleanor, which is super cool. But she speaks a language that Owen and Eleanor don't recognize, she dresses differently—and even her food looks unfamiliar. Owen and Eleanor decide to keep an eye on this new kid . . . but they aren't expecting her to catch them spying! *Owen and Eleanor Meet the New Kid* is a story about welcoming strangers and loving your neighbor— and maybe even discovering a new friend in the process.

ISBN: 978-1-5064-4845-9